The Creative Pen

An Anthology

By Students of Young Writers' Academy LLC

The Creative Pen
Short Stories of YWA Students
An Anthology

Christine T. Wade
Editor

DEDICATION

The Young Writers' Academy thanks and dedicates this book to the authors who contributed to this Anthology.

Contents
(In order of submission)

ACKNOWLEDGMENTS

I wish to thank the writers who submitted their creative work for the Anthology. As everyone knows, it is no small undertaking to invent characters and a plot to entertain an audience; let alone finish a story for publication.

The Anthology could not have been possible without the assistance of our fabulous instructors who facilitated the Young Writers' Academy "Get Published" classes in North Carolina, South Carolina and Washington.

Ultimately, none of the stories would be possible without the support and encouragement of the writers' parents. Thank you!

Christine Wade
Founder, Young Writers' Academy LLC

CORWIN SHORE
BIOGRPHY

Corwin Shore is 11 years old, and currently lives in

Waxhaw, North Carolina with his parents, 2 sisters, and

dog. He loves playing soccer, writing books, and playing

any sort of game.

The Tale of the Small Man and the Tall Man

By: Corwin Shore

Logan Miller woke up inside his mansion on the outside of New York City. He could see his garden from his room, fluttering with birds and insects. In the trees, he saw squirrels and chipmunks quarreling for the acorns he left out. He got up and stretched. Logan looked at his phone to check his calendar. He had nothing to do but practice hoops in the city. Logan was a star basketball player for the prosperous Brooklyn Nets, a six foot three point guard. He got changed into his workout clothes - Adidas everything. After he brushed his teeth and ate breakfast, he was ready to go.

At practice, Logan was working on his 3-pointers when Timmy Marlan, his best friend, walked in. Logan had just swooshed a three when Timmy took the ball and chucked it at the hoop across the gym. It gracefully arced through the air...hitting the ground about thirty meters short of the basket. Logan laughed.

Timmy, embarrassed, said "That was not the reason I came. I need you to help me test a magic trick."

Logan thought it would be some kind of card trick, so he agreed. Timmy pulled out a red and blue dotted wand, shouted something that Logan couldn't understand, and pointed the wand at him. Logan was about to laugh when a black ray shot out of the wand and hit him in the thigh. Logan winced at the short jab like feeling.

All of a sudden, he shrank to the size of his thigh. At first, Logan didn't realize what had happened.

"Wow, this is cool, but could you move my vision back to my head?"

Timmy, looking a bit nervous, said "Yea sure, but could you come to the next room?"

As Logan began to walk into the next room he realized what really happened. In a state of shock, he screamed and ran ahead to the room. There was a couch in the room. Timmy sat down easily, while Logan struggled to get up. When Logan was finally up, Timmy sighed and told Logan that he didn't think the trick would work and so didn't know exactly how to undo it. Logan got really mad and made Timmy promise he would find a way.

"Let's go to the science center and see what they can do" Timmy said hopefully.

Timmy picked Logan up and put him in his magic hat. The science center was only a ten minute drive from the gym, but to Logan, it seemed like an eternity. Not knowing where to go, they randomly chose the 11th floor and walked into the third door they saw. It was a large room with lots of test tubes, each filled with something different. There were also stacks of empty water bottles. Across the room, they noticed a scientist facing the other direction. A plaque on the desk in front of him read: Evan Siloman.

"You know that evil plan I was talking about?" the scientist barked into his phone.

Timmy looked astonished. He took Logan out of his hat and suggested Logan spy on the scientist.

Logan hid behind a box. Timmy silently walked out. Logan stayed standing by that box for 10 minutes while Evan continued talking. Logan learned that Evan was actually an evil scientist trying to take over the world. His plan was to put a secret potion in the water bottles and hand them out to people. Logan ran outside to tell Timmy. Evan's first target was a subway station.

The next day Timmy and Logan travelled to the station early in the morning. It turned out to be a private station. The security guard wouldn't let them pass.

"You need a membership to enter," the guard grunted. He pointed at a large white building, "You can get a membership there. You will receive it in 2 days."

Logan, who was watching it all from down below cringed. Finally, Logan spoke up, "Well, we need a membership today."

The guard looked surprised and looked around the room to find where the voice came from. Logan thought he would play a little game with him.

"I am a ghost of the station," Logan tried to sound ominous. "I was killed during the construction and have been haunting this place ever since." Logan knew it didn't flow with his previous statement, but he hoped it would work.

The guard shuddering with fear reached into his pocket and pulled out a card.

"H-here, y-you can have mine."

Timmy smiled and took it. "Thanks for your help."

Timmy scanned the card then walked in. Logan stuck by Timmy's leg, careful not to be seen. As they walked down the long barren hallway they could hear signs of people.

"Hot dogs. Hot dogs. Only $3.99," was one of the many calls from vendors.

They walked into a big room where it was bustling with people. The subway was just pulling up and a load of people got on and a load of people got off. Logan spotted Evan getting the train with his boxes of tainted water bottles.

"There!" Logan exclaimed, but Timmy was already on his way over there.

While they watched, Evan set up his stand in an empty corner on the platform and tried to get customers.

"Water bottles! Buy two get one free!"

Logan and Timmy stood near the stand trying to draw customer away from it. Then while they were distracted, a person bought one. He drank the whole thing in less than 5 sips. Timmy turned around and stared in horror. The man dropped the bottle and stood at attention. Logan saw Evan whisper something in the man's ear and the man started advertising the water. Then Logan realized the truth. Evan was mind-controlling whoever drank it.

Sure enough, more and more people started gravitating toward the stand. More and more people were getting mind-controlled. Timmy realized this too and told

Logan that they needed a plan. After debating, they came up with the following plan. Since Evan was drinking a normal water bottle, Logan would steal all of the poison water. He would bring them back and Timmy, with his magic wand, would group all of the poison into one ball which Logan would then throw into Evan's bottle. Then Evan will be mine-controlled by Timmy.

Carefully Logan retrieved all of the water bottles. Timmy shouted something and little green droplets emerged from the plastic bottles. Timmy gathered them into a fist sized ball and handed it to Logan.

"Be very careful," Timmy warned.

Logan took the ball and like shooting game winning 3 pointers made it into the water bottle. Evan was packing up because he had no water left. When he took a sip of water he dropped everything and stood at attention. Everyone else returned to normal.

"Now the final touch," Timmy said. "Abracadabra" and pointed the wand at Logan. A white ray shot out and hit Logan who returned to normal size. He was at his basketball game the next day and won the game with a last second 3-pointer. Legend has it that Evan is still at the station today.

MARIA MATTEI
BIOGRAPHY

Maria Mattei is 12 years old and in the 7th grade within the Voice Charter School in NYC. Maria is originally from Brazil, but currently lives in Long Island City, NY. She is always looking for a place to find a new story!

Moving On

By: Maria Mattei

My heart fell and apparently so did my legs. My face became as pale as a vampire on a full moon during a Halloween night. I made myself a river but I couldn't find a bridge to cross it. I guess I forgot to build one because I was so busy trying to avoid drowning under waves of sadness and anger. I leaned over. Somehow my fist curled up into a ball, my face became as red as a brick. My blood felt like a witch was cooking it to eat for dinner and was adding some jalapeños. I couldn't see it but I knew there were many bumps where my veins should be.

Suddenly my heart sank even more, now it was to my toes. It was my fault. If I had done it differently, I wouldn't be suffering. If only I had…

"STOOOOPPPP!" Something howled. "I'm a

spirit. I'm your mother's spirit." It added. "And I'm telling you to stop blaming yourself. It's not your fault!"

"What do you mean it's not my fault? If I hadn't left her..."

"NO! What did I tell you?" You could have done it differently but the ending of a book never changes, no matter how many twists and turns, it all leads up to that one ending."

I refused to agree with the spirit, but maybe deep down inside...

Suddenly swirls started to fill the room; it kind of looked like the flash-back scenes you would see in a movie. My brain started to hurt because of my dizziness. I felt the gentle breath of the spirit sitting on my shoulder. My mouth was dry and empty. It felt like I needed something sweet. Now that I think about it, my life could use something sweet in it too. I wondered, as I looked at the swirls and layers of blurry things, if I'd been dreaming or imagining everything that was going on. I forced myself a pinch. It didn't work. Nothing happened. This meant that it was probably real. I looked over my shoulder and asked the spirit:

"What's going on?"

"I'm going to show you what would have happened if you had done anything different!" She answered.

"Wouldn't it just be easier for you to tell me?"

"Would you believe me if I did?"

"Good point." I assured her.

After a while, the room became into focus again. But, what got me confused was that we were in the same room that we were in before all the swirly swirls happened.

"I thought you said you were gonna show me what would have happened if I'd done things differently? I don't know if you noticed but we are in the same place" I said in an obvious tone.

"No duh Sherlock!" She rudely replied.

"We are not at the same place. We're in the past of a different dimension," she then added.

"Oh, so that's not really me?" I said pointing to an exact copy of me.

"Well kind of… It's you in the past from another dimension."

"Oh, yeah that clears it up" I said sarcastically.

"I know it's confusing but it doesn't really matter, so if you can just be QUIET, it would really help."

We watched me stay with my mom, and not leave her side. It was weird because I was there but the other "me" couldn't hear me. I did stay with my mom and she didn't die, at least I thought she hadn't died. We watched my mom sleep. I looked at the spirit and opened my mouth to tell her *I* was right. But then I noticed that my mom's chest stopped going up and down. I went to check her pulse… nothing. As I placed my ear on her warm chest I couldn't hear any pounding. I felt her hands, they were ice cold. I turned to the spirit and said "My — my — mom is — er — gone — again."

"I'm sorry I just wanted —"

"YOU JUST WANTED TO WHAT? MAKE ME SEE MY MOM DIYING ALL OVER AGAIN? IS IT SOMEHOW PLEASING SEEING ME SUFFER?"

"I didn't want for you to suffer. I just wanted to show you how it wouldn't make any difference if you'd stayed with your mom, or left her! If anything, I was trying to help you!" the spirit whimpered as its eyes began to fill with tears.

"Look I'm sorry. I — er— didn't want to make you cry." I apologized.

The spirit explained to me that in this version my mom was sick and she didn't tell me.

I couldn't believe it. The spirit of my mom was right the whole time even if I had stayed with my mom, eventually she would die!

I remember exactly how my mom died...

It was an afternoon and I got invited to a party that I really wanted to go because all my friends were going to be there. My dad was on a business trip, so it was just me, my mom, and Riley, my dog. My mom wouldn't let me go because she didn't want to be alone. My mom didn't like to be home alone because both her mother and father died when they were by themselves. So, I decided to sneak out when my mom was taking a shower. I came back early because I felt bad. When I laid my eyes on my mom, she was lying on the floor. I immediately thought someone must have sneaked inside the house and killed her! There was a bullet mark on my mom's forehead and blood dripping from it. I wished they would've left the gun on the floor so the police could do their whole fingerprint thingamajig and find out who did it. They would've been able to find out who killed my mom. I wondered how my dad would react to this. He would be devastated! I wondered if it would be weird if he found someone else. I wondered if we were gonna act like those books and movies where the dad becomes all tough with the son and eventually their relationship falls apart. If I lost my dad I would have no one to comfortably talk to. That was not going to happen. No way was I gonna let it.

I heard a poof. And the spirit was gone.

I went back to my dimension at the correct time. Throughout the time were the only thing I could see was swirls and blurs, I thought about what I had just seen. I was trying to process it all. It all came back to me. The feeling of loss and loneliness.

I guess that the spirit was right all along! Some things just happen because they are meant to happen! My mom's death was and still is the worst thing that has ever happened to me! I can't imagine how my life is going to be now. There's only one thing that now I know for sure: Life knows what it's doing. Trust it! Everything will end up fine in the end! After all you can't change the end of a book.

ELOISE SAX
BIOGRAPHY

Eloise recently turned 13 years old, and is in the 7th

grade. She lives with her parents, cat Emily, dog India,

one hen, and her 60-gallon fresh-water aquarium in

Seattle, WA. She enjoys reading, writing, music and art,

dancing and marine biology.

Yuki's Quest for Light

By Eloise Sax

I dedicate my story to my family -- for pushing me to write, and for being there. And to my friend, Sydney, for inspiring me and introducing me to Percy Jackson.

In the world of Kamigami No Sekai, the goddesses slumbered away, unknowing of what was to happen. Kaibutsu, who kidnapped Hikari out of anger for nearly blinding her at a young age, scanned the row of goddesses, poorly passing over each. Finally, she found the goddess she was looking for. She was just about to float off the cloud bank when Tenshi awoke. Tenshi peacefully glided over towards Kaibutsu and then gave a chilling shriek, awakening the others. Kaibutsu used this chance to slink away to Kokishin, the darkest place in the Underground, and her home. The goddesses nervously shifted, waiting for Jinsaku, the Victory Goddess, to stir. The moment she awoke, she was bombed with a load of

Questions,

"How will we help Hikari?"

"I'm not sure, Okasan."

"What about that child of yours?"

"Yuki-Chan? I suppose…"

After the goddesses seemed satisfied with their surely victorious plan, they sent Heirula to fetch Yuki. Heirula gently flittered down, scanning the rich, silk-like green land, elegantly folding into hills of emerald. A few houses dotted the countryside, all nearly identical but for one; a pretty white house with shutters, the color of sunshine, and a blacked-tiled roof. A young girl was sitting on the lawn, serenely plucking flowers. "I'm looking for…uh…Yuki-Tenshi-chan!" "Ah. Her aunt?"

"Um, yes. Her aunt Heiwa."

The girl in the field stood up and bowed respectfully. Heiwa smiled.

"Right this way, Your Greatness."

"Heiwa is fine."

"YUKI-CHAAAN!!" The girl yelled.

"WHAAAT ODAYANKA-SAAN?" Came a voice, shouting just as loud, "I'M BUSY!"

"YOUR OBA-SAN HEIWA IS HERE!"

Yuki's voice fell silent. A minute later, she came down, an old T-shirt and a pair of athletic shorts adorning her body. She, too, bowed and then hugged Heiwa.

"You look flustered, Oba-San."

"Hikari is missing!!!"

"Oh, my gosh!!!"

"Your mother has a plan. Take my mirror and your mother's dagger. You must work quickly, as we only have one day before the world suffers. Kaibutsu's lair is in Kokoshin. Now, hurry. You weren't named bravery for nothing. We'll be watching over you. I promise."

"Okay. I trust you, "Yuki's small hand closed over the mirror, a sense of peace settling throughout her body. "For the goddesses!"

She bolted out of the house, her steady pace kicking in. She ran the two miles to the edge of town. Now, the only things keeping her from getting to the Undergrounds were the huge rock ledge and the fire seas. "Oh Sorra, Sacred Fire Goddess, oh Mizu, Sacred Water Goddess, please let me survive." And then, bravely, she lept.

She didn't feel the burning sensation that was common among the swimmers. In a few moments, she had swum the length of the salty river. She clambered up the rock ledge, and scaled the hills on the island. Then, she crept over to the gaping maw that leads to the Underground. She sprang through easily, ricocheting on the walls.

"Hikari, I'm coming." She muttered, following

the tiny pinprick of light.

"Who'sss there?" A voice hissed.

"Um… My n-name's Yuki."

"Bravery? Heh. Cute."

"TAKE THAT!!!" Yuki pointed a mirror

towards Kaibutsu, and the Sun Goddess, while in

a cage, could still use her powers, so she pointed

some light straight at the mirror, and the light

bounced into Kaibutsu's face, temporarily fully

blinding her. She screamed, clawing the air.

"OW! Gasp! MY WING!!!" Yuki stared at her

torn wing, its sharp edge gleaming as though it

were glass. Yuki couldn't waste any time howling

about her wing, so she gritted her teeth and

started picking the lock on Hikari's cage. Soon,

the goddess was free. All the goddesses reveled, and Yuki was looked upon as a hero.

*Okasan is the formal way of addressing your mother.

A Violet Touched World
By: Helena Cirian

"Leave me alone!" I cried over my shoulder, galloping into the woods that were my home for now. I heaved a sigh of relief as the raptors flew away. I shook out my mane and looked over my lithe, black body. The cuts on my back from their sharp talons were bleeding and my long black tail was tangled with leaves and twigs. With a snort of disgust, I trotted into my clearing, and started to reflect on my situation again.

I had come from a huge herd that lived in a secluded valley. My brother, Diamond, was always teasing me that my name, Violet, did not match my black body with its contrasting white socks and white star. With a spark of satisfaction, I remembered how my mother Lyssa, had told me that my name represented the ancient herd spirit of perseverance.

A month ago, Diamond and I had gone down to the river in our valley, right after a big storm to search for any trace of our mother, Lyssa, who had disappeared a month earlier. As I leaned out precariously over the water's edge, I lost my footing and fell into the deep turbulent water. I was swept away, nature trying to hurt me with everything she had. After a while, I ended up here, wherever here was. Huge woods, grassy fields, but no river, scared and with no way to return home. I was trying to work up the courage to leave the woods to search for my herd.

Suddenly, I heard a low growling. A huge cat was slinking through the leaves, tracking me. The cat lunged, and I reared up at it. It snarled and backed off, and then I realized it was calling for reinforcements. Knowing that I was no match for more of them, I cantered out of my clearing, pushing aside the leaves and branches in my way. Finally, I stumbled out of the woods. A little way down, three large cats bounded out. With one look, I galloped across the plains.

"Eat my dust!" I called back, knowing that they would not be able to catch me. I ran for the rest of the day until the sky turned dark. Looking around, I spotted a small hill, and climbed it, searching for a sheltered dip in the ground where I could sleep. None. Nowhere.

"Ugh, how much worse can my luck get?" I asked irritably. I trotted down the hill to an outcropping of rocks where I would get a little protection from the wind. I tucked my legs under me, and fell asleep. I awoke at dawn and trotted back up the hill to see if anything looked different in the daylight.

"Wait!" I gasped my head shooting up to take a better look. In the distance, a large stretch of mountains loomed. One of them was unmistakably the tallest peak of the mountains I woke up to every morning with my herd.

"Yes! I found it! I know where to go; Diamond, I'm coming home!" I yelled, and then reared in anger at myself. If you learned anything out here, it was that you couldn't attract more attention than you could handle. Sure enough, the cats that had been following me came into view. I reared, coming to land inches from one's face. It backed off, and for a moment I thought I won. Then another one leaped on me from behind, and clawed at my shoulders, leaving deep cuts. Thinking quickly, I dropped to the ground, and rolled, crushing the cat under me. It yowled, and I leaped up as the rest started retreating. Finally, they all slunk away, and I heaved a sigh of relief as they disappeared from sight. Then I walked back to the rocks to rest and recover.

I knew I should leave the hill, as the cats had made enough noise to alert every predator in the area, but

I could barely move. The pain from the scrapes on my back were overwhelming my senses, and it was all I could do to limp to the shelter of the rocks. I settled down as best I could, and tucked my nose down, sheltering from the pain.

I stayed there for the rest of the day, and into the night. The pain in my shoulders was easing, and I carefully got to my hooves, and sighed in relief as the rest of the red haze faded away. I stretched, and set off at a brisk trot, extremely aware that I was leaving any shelter behind until I reached home. Even with the darkness, I knew the direction of my mountain, and trotted towards it until I could go no further. Then I found a small patch of bushes, and lay down, trying to make myself as small as possible for shelter.

I slept peacefully, until I woke to a bone-chilling hiss. I leaped up, letting out a shrill whinny as I saw a huge snake writhing its way towards me. I jumped up, and whinnied again as it hissed. I charged it, and at the last possible moment, I jumped over it, running once again towards my mountain. I was feeling much better, as I was mostly free of pain, and heading towards home.

Suddenly I saw a sight that stopped me in my tracks – a human! Why would a human be out here? I reared, whinnying a challenge. The human took a step forward, then another, and another. Slowly, it walked closer, until it was no more than a step away. It raised its arm, until its hand came close to touching my muzzle. I tilted my head to the side, completely baffled. What was it expecting? Then with a start, I saw something that made my heart skip a beat. A strand of glistening black tail waving around the human's boot, the exact shade and length as my mother's! I jerked my muzzle up and bit the human's hand. I stared into its eyes for a minute, teeth still clamped on its hand. I let go as it yelled in pain, and reared up, and started running for home. I galloped all day and all night, until I came to the familiar entrance to my valley. I started forward as I saw who was coming out of it.

"Diamond!" I called, and he started trotting, then galloping towards me.

"Violet?" he called sounding amazed. "You're alive! Thank the ancestors; the whole herd was lost without you! *I* was lost without you." He reached me, and pressed his muzzle against, my cheek.

"I'm so happy to be home. You have no idea how much I've been through." As I was talking, the rest of the herd started spilling through the passage to see what the commotion was.

"Violet?" Someone called.

"You're back!" Said someone else.

"I thought you were dead!" Suddenly, everyone was crowding around me, telling me how glad they were that I was back.

"I'm here." I whispered, feeling my perseverance grow as I was surrounded by my herd, feeling safer than I ever imagined I would, I steeled myself, and said, "I also found evidence of Lyssa's fate."

CONNOR HENDERSON MOORE
BIOGRAPHY

Connor lives in North Carolina and currently lives in Charlotte, North Carolina. He will be going into third grade in the fall. Connor lives with his mother, father and brother. Connor Henderson Moore hobbies include racing, baseball and eating pizza with his family. He hopes he will be a baseball player when he becomes an adult.

<u>Fight!</u>
By: Connor Henderson Moore

A big argument was happening in Spain. It was with Spain and U.S. Henric, John, Isabella and Cary had to live in Spain because Spain kicked them out of the U. S. Their land was taken over because Spain wanted to have people go to work for them.

Henric, John, Isabella said, "Let's fight."

Spain's leader George said, "Sure ready to go down?"

The people of Spain said, "Ha ha ha ha!"

Henric exclaimed, "Oh who cares about that, you are going down! We're going to win again Spain!

Bang! The war had begun and everybody shot their guns again and again until Spain surrendered because George was gone so Spain had to give the USA land back.

KILEY SANDRIDGE
BIOGRAPHY

Kiley Elizabeth Sandridge was born in Norfolk, Virginia. She lives in Charlotte with her parents and two brothers and is in the third grade at Hawk Ridge Elementary. She has enjoyed writing stories for a long time. In the future, she plans to become a teacher and a spy. Kiley is also an artist and hopes to become a black belt in taekwondo.

Zombie Invasion

By: Kiley Sandridge

I dedicate my story to my teacher for inspiring me to write a really great tale.

I knew I was late so I needed to rush. No bus. Nobody in the car line. When I finally walked into the school building, everything was different. The Safety Patrol didn't yell at me for being late. They simply weren't there. My teacher wasn't hanging out her door, watching for my arrival. She was gone too. I just thought that I was really late. I rushed to my class without looking around at other classrooms for teachers or students. Finally I stood outside the door of my classroom, peering in through the small window in the door. It was then that I knew something was wrong, very wrong. The door was locked and the lights were out. I was looking around for any possible way in when I saw something zoom across the room. What was that? I

wondered. Next I noticed writing on the big chalkboard.
It read:

I am Mr. Zombiebones. I'm a zombie without any

friends. And I will turn everyone into zombies.

P.S. I HATE pink!

"Oh, no!" I said aloud. "I need to stop Mr.
Zombiebones!"

For a moment I couldn't move—or think! I was so
worried. Then I remembered the writing on the
chalkboard and got an idea. If Mr. Zombiebones hates the
color pink, I needed to find something pink—and fast!

"School's over at four o-clock," I thought to myself,
"so I can go to the store during school time." Thankfully
my mom gave me my allowance the night before so I had
just enough to buy something that might help me save
my friends and my school.

I rushed out the school door and ran like I was in the Olympics! When I got to the parking lot, I wished I could hop in a car because I was so tired and out of breath. Instead I ran to the store down the street called Best Home. My mom had taken me there once and I remembered the aisle where the pink toys were placed. As it happened, I liked pink!

"Hi," I said to the cashier when I entered. Then I ran straight for the aisle P for pink. I began my search for just the right item. The bell rang at the door of the store as someone entered. I hoped it would be my best friend Nate and looked up. I couldn't believe my eyes!

It was Mr. Zombiebones! He was after me! I tried not to scream and quickly looked for a place to hide. I hurried to the furniture section and made a little fort of chairs. When it was done, I crawled in and put a pillow in front of my hideout. I peeked through a crack in the chairs and watched Mr. Zombiebones. He couldn't find me, got frustrated and left! When he was gone I crawled out of the chair fort and ran back to aisle P. You know what? I found the perfect thing! It was pink slime! I grabbed it and went to the check out. I guess the cashier hid from creepy Mr. Zombiebones because she was still human.

"Fifty cents," the cashier said, looking to be sure Mr. Zombiebones was gone for good. I reached in my pocket and pulled out a dollar and quickly put it on the counter. With my fifty cents in change and my slime, I ran out. Being desperate can make you do crazy things. I decided I HAD to have a car to beat Mr. Zombiebones back to the school. Searching the store parking lot, I found keys on the ground next to a beat up blue four-door. I had to borrow that car! How could I possibly drive it? As it happened there was a kid's booster seat in the back. I unlocked the car and moved the booster to the driver's seat. This helped me see out the window shield. Next I found two water bottles on the floor of the car and taped one to each foot. Now I was able to reach the gas and brake pedals! I hit the road and was on my way to the school when I saw a figure by the road. It wasn't Mr. Zombiebones, thank goodness. It was my best friend Nate!

"Get in, Nate," I told him. "We have to save the school!"

"Mason! You're safe!" Nate said, climbing in next to me. "What's the slime for?"

"I'll explain later," I answered.

But it was too late! Mr. Zombiebones appeared suddenly on the road, right in front of us. I put on the brakes and the car came to a complete stop. And I stopped Mr. Zombiebones too! Want to know how? I climbed on top of the car and opened the slime. I dumped all of it on Mr. Zombiebones.

"Ahhhhhh!" he started to scream, "No, not PINK!" I think I saw him getting shorter or was I getting taller? Then I realized there was a growing puddle under him. He was melting! Then I realized another thing…the time! I looked at my watch. It was nearly four o'clock. So I got back in the car and drove to the school where my mom was waiting for me. And there were other cars and students too. Everyone was back again.

By that evening, everyone knew about the secret encounter Nate and I had with Mr. Zombiebones. It was caught on camera and sent to the television station. Nate and I were on the news! As exciting as that was, I knew that Mr. Zombiebones melted a lonely, friendless zombie and he might be back. Nate and I came up with a plan.

For the next three days, we left a message for Mr. Zombiebones on the chalkboard in the classroom. On the morning of the fourth day, he had responded! He wrote in chalk:

I am Mr. Zombiebones and I have always wanted a friend. Now I have two. When you write me I become a happy zombie and I will make sure no bad zombies ever come to your school!

Nate and I were so excited! We told the news reporter and they shared our story with the world. It's a good thing to make friends—even with a zombie!

LUCAS GROTZKE
BIOGRAPHY

Lucas Grotzke was born in and currently lives in Charlotte, NC. He attends Myers Park Traditional Elementary School as a First Grader in Ms. Endermann's class. Lucas lives with his mom, dad and big sister, Camyrn. The knight's Battle is Lucas' first published short story. Outside of school, Lucas enjoys playing baseball, basketball, water skiing and snowboarding.

The Knight's Battle

By: Lucas Grotzke

One dark night the dragon took the gold from the castle. He took the gold because he wanted to be rich.

The Knight said, "Who goes there?" The knight pulled his sword and started to fight the dragon.

The dragon blew his fire. Finally the knight got his gold back and won the battle. And…they became good friends and shared the gold!

LIAM ANTHONY WADE
BIOGRAPHY

Liam Wade was born in and currently lives in Charlotte, NC. He attends St. Matthew's Elementary School as a First Grader. Liam lives with his mom, dad and big sister, Natalie. The Creepy Night is Liam's first published short story. Outside of school, Liam enjoys playing baseball, karate, flag football, video games and hanging out with friends.

THE CREEPY NIGHT

By: Liam Wade

It was a spooky night. The wind was roaring outside Liam's house as he watched *Star Wars* and ate candy. Suddenly, the lights went out! Liam was so scared as he got up from the couch to see what had happened. Then, there was a scratching noise at the front door! Liam nervously opened the door. He giggled with relief; it was just his friend Matty. But as Liam threw open the door, he screamed in terror. Matty was covered in blood and his shirt was ripped to shreds.

"Matty," Liam stammered, "why is your face all blue?"

MREHHGGRRNG!!! He moaned in reply and began walking into the house very weirdly.

"Zombie!" cried Liam, and he raced down the hall like a mad lion. He grabbed a knife for protection and turned to face the zombie at the door. But to his surprise, the zombie was laughing! Then he saw five other friends huddled outside laughing loudly.

Angrily, Liam slammed the door. It was all a joke!

After his heart stopped beating so fast, Liam opened the door and invited his friends in to watch the rest of *Star Wars.* What a crazy night!

The End

JJ SCHWIEBERT
BIOGRAPHY

JJ is a 7 year old boy who just finished 1st grade at Our Lady of the Lake School in Seattle, WA. His story is dedicated to Garfield.

GARFIELD SEES DINOSAURES

By: JJ SCHWIEBERT

Once upon a time Garfield was watching TV when Jon came into the room. Jon said, "Garfield, I wonder what it would be like to travel through time."

"I like that," said Garfield.

"BARK! BARK!" went Odie.

"I'm going to go torment the dog next door," Garfield said.

Garfield had lied to Jon, but Jon did not know. Garfield went to Rome. It took him five minutes to walk to Rome. When he got to Rome, he went to the time machine shop and bought one. He bought one that had to be built, so he took it home to build it. It took forever to build it.

When the time machine was ready, Garfield

jumped into it. It was a long, twisty slide. It made

Garfield dizzy. It was really dark in there. He shot

through at the speed of light.

When Garfield landed he was in the time of the

dinosaurs.

"OOF!" said Garfield.

It was SO! SO! SO! SO! SO! SO! SO! Cool!

"What's this?" said Garfield.

"Oooooooooowwwwwwwwww!!!!!!!" He yelled.

Then Odie came through the time machine. Then

Garfield jumped on to a Spinosaurus.

"Giddy up!" yelled Garfield. Then he ran back to

the time machine.

ANABEL CAROLINE TRZNADEL

BIOGRAPHY

Annabel Caroline Trznadel was born in North Carolina and currently lives in Charlotte. She attends Myers Park Traditional School and will be going into first grade this fall. Annabel lives with her mom, dad, brother (William). Annabel loves art, reading, dancing and swimming. Annabel participates in soccer. She hopes to be a teacher when she grows up.

MAGIC OBJECTS

By: Anabel Caroline Trznadel

One sunny day Jack Frost took the magic objects from the fairies while they were sleeping. The magic objects were a bell, seashell, and a pearl.

The bell alerts bad guys. The seashell helps heal. The pearl helps free the mermaid.

Jack Frost said," I want to take over the world.

The fairies had a plan. Jack Frost was in his chair. When Jack Frost was telling the goblins to close the door into the castle. They went into the room. They got back their magic objects, but Jack Frost did not see them.

PAYTON MAJORS

BIOGRAPHY

Payton Majors was born in Charlotte, North Carolina, where she currently lives. She attends Myers Park Traditional School and will be going into the 5th grade this fall. Payton lives with her mom, dad, two sisters and her pets. Payton Majors has written "Dust and Depression," "Dust Poem" and "The Wonderland." She hopes to be a poet when she becomes an adult. She also loves karate and plays piano.

THE WONDERLAND

By: Payton Majors

"Get off, get off!" I yelled at my little sister, Hallie. "I have to go!" I screeched. I ran out the door, and behind me I heard my sister shout "Wait, Mia!" I darted into a nearby cave, hoping for a place to hide.

Everything immediately went dark as I fell through a hole in the floor of the cave. I landed on my feet and immediately fell down. I looked around but couldn't see a thing.

"U-uh are y-you okay?" a small voice stammered. I looked up as my eyes adjusted to the dark.

"Ahhh!" I backed away on all four arms and legs. I stared at the hideous creature standing before me. "W-who are you?" I managed to stammer through my cracked lips and dried throat. He cleared his throat.

"They call me Shrekton. Now come along. We need to get you back to your home. You fell through a portal into my world. We call it Wonderland."

He got me on my feet and dragged me along. "Where are we going?" I asked slowly.

"To the King's castle," he responded. "Behind it is a secret way to get you back home. Here, let me explain -" A giant rock cut him off and knocked me down. "Oof!" He rushed me up off of the ground. "Are you okay?"

"Yeah," I sighed with impatience. There was a rumble. "WATCH OUT!" I screamed. A big boulder hurled toward us and we started to run away.

"The King knows you're here! He forbids humans."

"Okay, so how exactly do you know he knows that I'm
here?" I asked as I panted

"He's the King of Rock, so he sent that boulder to us to
drive you away." We continued to run. Luckily the
castle was close by, so we go there minutes later.

Shrekton pulled me onto a metal platform. "Close your
eyes," he whispered. I squeezed my eyes shut
obediently. When I opened them I was in my own room.
I was back home.

EMMA CATES
BIOGRAPHY

Emma Cates was born in North Carolina and currently lives in Charlotte, North Carolina. She attends Myers Park Traditional School and will be going into the third grade this fall. Emma lives with her mom, dad, brother and soon-to-be sister. Emma Cates has written The Unicorn, Super Hero Academy and The Green Goblin. She hopes to be a teacher when she becomes an adult. Emma loves to play all sports and she loves to travel.

THE UNICORN

By Emma Cates

One warm sunny day a little unicorn was playing in his yard. Suddenly he heard a big BANG! So he started running. The path he was running on led him to the woods. He ran so fast that he ran into a tree. Suddenly he lost his way. Then he heard something.

It was a voice. The voice said, "HELP, HELP"! Then he saw a fairy. Behind her was a monster. The fairy flew over and hid behind the unicorn.

When the monster could not find the fairy he said, "I will be back."

The fairy said, "Sorry if I scared you. My name is Lydia. Thanks for letting me hide behind you!"

"Hello, my name is Max," said the unicorn. "I lost my way. Will you help me get home?"

Lydia said that she would, of course, help him. They started looking for the unicorn's home. Finally, they found a place that Max recognized. Then the monster jumped out of a tree. It had been following them.

Lydia and Max were very scared. "Quick, come this way," said Max. They started running towards Max's home. The monster was chasing them the whole way, growling, panting and drooling. He wanted to eat Max and Lydia! After running for a long time, Max saw his home. Lydia and Max quickly ran inside and locked the door. The monster was furious! He started to bang on the door to try to get in. In the meantime, Max and Lydia snuck out of the back window and tip toed to the front of the house. The monster did not see them so they snuck up behind him and whacked him over the head

with a frying pan. The monster cried out in pain and fell

to the ground. He scrambled to his feet and ran away as

fast as he could never to be seen or heard from again!

NORAH BOLEWITZ
BIOGRAPHY

Norah Bolewitz was born in North Carolina and currently

lives in Charlotte. She attends Myers Park

Traditional School and will be going into first grade this

fall. Norah lives with her mom, dad, brothers

Holden and James, and her dog, Stella. Norah loves art

and often draws pictures and writes notes,

mailing them to family members that she loves. Norah

participates in karate, dance and gymnastics. She

hopes to be a ballet teacher when she grows up.

PUPPY AND ME

By Norah Bolewitz

One sunny day the puppy wanted to go on a walk. The girl did not want to go on a walk. She said, "I have too much stuff to do."

The puppy barked. The girl yelled, "no!" After she did all her stuff she took the puppy on a walk. The puppy felt happy.

She took the puppy to the dog park! The puppy ran with her friends. They chased a Frisbee. The puppy barked "bye" to her friends. It was a good day.

HOLDEN BOLEWITZ
BIOGRAPHY

Holden Bolewitz was born in North Carolina and currently lives in Charlotte. He attends Myers Park Traditional School and will be going into the third grade this fall. Holden lives with his mom, dad, siblings Norah and James, and his dog, Stella. Holden likes to write short stories and has written Tornadoes and a Pokémon book. Holden participates in karate and baseball. He hopes to be a policeman when he becomes an adult.

THE DARK MONKEY

By Holden Bolewitz

Baby King Monkey was a nice baby. But an evil sorcerer cast a spell on him one gloomy day.

"HAHAHAHAHAHAHAHAHA," said King Monkey and jumped out of his house. "Victory to me! I'm going to steal some money from the city," said King Monkey.

Back at his house, Ninja Monkey, his brother, was getting ready for battle! "For once, King Monkey will be defeated by me! I will save the city! But first I need to find a team," said Ninja Monkey.

BRRRINNNG!

"Whaaaaat?" said King Monkey. "Oh, it's the telephone. Who is this? Blah, blah, blah. Ninja Monkey! Impossible! You've got to be KIDDING. I'm hanging up right now. Oh, and one more thing, I'm going to be RICH," said King Monkey.

"Like he really is. Never" said Ninja Monkey.

BRRRRINNNNG. "It's Ninja Monkey again! Hey Ninja Monkey, I have the greediest wolves and I'm sending them out today. Bye, bye" said King Monkey.

"Noooooo," said Ninja Monkey. "That's it! I'm going in the castle. Come here horse. Run, run, run! I'm here. Oh no! Guards! Shhh, horse, stay here." Hi-ya! Pow! BAM! SLAP! "I'm done, there is the gold! Space ship!

I'm loading all the gold into you! Here, get in, I'm
done!"

Now King Monkey is nice. The money is
back with the city. "Yay, King Monkey."

The End.

DESTINED ONES

By: Yasmine Luong

I dedicate my book to my wonderful, loving and caring family. My younger sister, mother, and father.

Lightning streaked everywhere and dark clouds were traveling to every corner of the sky. "It's very stormy out mum. Do you think pa will be alright?"

Farthia glared at her daughter with such a gaze that could melt a door. "For the LAST time, your father will be fine!" her mother shouted angrily. With a snarl, she continued cleaning the kitchen.

Diane opened her mouth, wanting to apologize, but shut it quickly. She walked out the door and was welcomed by a chilly breeze. She followed a dusty path up to the tallest hill, which overlooked the city to gather some water from a well. Her thin fingers clutched the pail tightly for every step she took. Along the way, the rain would pour rapidly down her dress making her feel miserable. As she made her way to the top of the hill, she noticed an old lady slumping on the stony well.

"Hello Diane Rose. I have been waiting for you," the woman eerily spoke. Each word the woman uttered sent small stabs up her arm. She shivered in uneasiness of the peculiar woman.

"W-who are y-you?" she managed to say.
"Whom, are you?" the woman echoed back.
"I am here to get water for my mum." She tried to state firmly. Her grip on the pail seemed to loosen with every word she said. Diane finally couldn't bear the unseen pain the woman brought her any more. The pail she was carrying fell and shattered into a million pieces. In mere

moments, the strange woman morphed into a strikingly beautiful witch. Her head told her to turn towards her small village and her feet turned ever so slowly. Her village was shriveling up and people were running around frantically. She collapsed on the path feeling torn between her real thoughts. When she found the strength to stand up she realized the scene was an illusion. She fought the urge to cry and faced the witch. "If I am alive you will never take my village down," she shakily exclaimed. With a flourish, she ran down the hill, across the dusty path, and past several vendors to her destination. She knocked and nervously waited for an answer.

"Hello? Diane? What's wrong?" her best friend, Carol asked.

"I need help, remember the legend about the Gray Witch? It's real and her next step is here!" Carol's face lit up with concern. She wrapped her arms around Diane and led her inside to warm up by the fireplace. The heat from the fire calmed Diane down and made her think clearly. She finally spoke to Carol clearly about the past events that had happened that day.

Carol at last shrieked and called her twin brother to listen to the story. "I find that hard to believe." he stammered. "I'm going to check the library for some information on this witch," Dean replied nervously. After a while, Dean emerged with several articles and books containing information. The most accurate article read:

Date: March 20, 1500

An unknown figure approached the town of Winkelsburg and created a disastrous weather event. Our town was nearly destroyed. I was the only survivor. The key to stopping this witch is to go to the Temple of Aragon and retrieve the ancient scroll. This is the only way to

defeat this witch. Ibid you farewell.

Lady Smith of Templeton

Diane was puzzled and tried to recall this somehow familiar name. The idea popped into her head as quick as a cheetah. "Guys, Lady Smith was the founder of our house..." she trailed off anxiously. All of them huddled together and decided what to do with this information.

"We should run away with our families and find refuge elsewhere," Dean suggested.

"That would be running away from our problems and you both know that I would never agree to that," Diane stated firmly.

Dean sighed and rubbed his temples. "What choice do we

have?"

Carol pleaded mercifully. Diane grabbed ahold of her

friends and begged for them to listen to her reasoning. At

the end one choice was made, they would save their

village and retrieve the scroll to defeat the Gray Witch.

Chapter Two

Carol began drying her tears and helped Dean pack all

their bags. Diane fumbled with the lock on the door and

felt a creeping pain take over her body. What if they

couldn't do this? They were children after all. A gust of

wind seemed to howl in agreement at her. "Let's go, I

don't want to see the witch on the way out," Diane called

feverishly.

The sky was beginning to darken and wolves howled in

the distance. The three of them crept farther into the

village until they reached the forest. "This is it," Diane

muttered. Carol ushered them further into the trees.

Diane followed Carol and Dean deeper across a lake and

into a cave. Her eyes were drooping and her feet ached,

she knew she had to rest. As the twins pushed through,

she tripped over a tree root and lay, sprawling across the

forest floor. Her surroundings seemed to become a

blur and she slowly fell into a deep sleep. Without any

knowledge, of the loss of their dear friend the siblings

found a small grove in which to rest their souls. Night

quickly became day and realization came to find Carol

and Dean.

"Where is Diane?" Carol wearily asked. Dean looked

half-asleep and half-awake pushed on his glasses. "I'm

not quite sure, we should continue or journey. The most

sensible thing to do is let her find her way back to our

camp site," he went on with not a single amount of

sadness. Carol grabbed her brother's shoulders and

tightened her grip. "We need to find Diane," Carol angrily stated. Her brother slipped out of her threatening grasp and let out a long sigh.

"I understand you worry about Diane, but we need to continue this journey," Dean sadly explained.

Carol began sniffling and gathered her small bookbag. "I'm sorry brother. You're going to have to go without me," Carol murmured under her breath. The two siblings walked off into different directions and to their doom.

A robin was chirping a lovely song and the sun was streaming down ever so lightly down on the forest trees. Deer's were roaming on several patches of dewy grass. A creek was flowing with fresh water from the sparkling waterfall. Time seemed to stand still as Diane yawned and stretched, awake from her long slumber. As soon as she realized what had happened the day before she collapsed on the ground sobbing. An hour passed by and she decided to be brave and face her fears. After refilling her food supplies she planned a plan to find the Temple of Aragon and save her village. She made it to a grove of trees that had the remains of a burnt-out fire. She recognized an encyclopedia from Dean's bookshelf behind a bush and was relieved. Finding her friends wasn't part of her plan, but she was glad to know they were close by.

A rustling and a scream frightened Diane greatly. She followed the strange series of sounds and came across the Temple of Aragon. "You're here!" an excited voice yelled. Carol came bounding towards her, her curly, orange hair flopped around. "I knew you would find the way" she giggled happily. Diane smiled and shook

shook her head no and stood behind the witch. "Very well, you can join the rest of your friends," she commanded. Diane followed the witch into a small room. As soon as the witch left she called upon her friends.

"I figured out why the scroll was blank," she explained. She whispered the explanation into her friend's ears and all of them began to get excited. The three children huddled together and thought of all the things they did together, their memories, and their strong bond. The witch stared in horror as she was disappearing slowly.

"Nooooo!" the Gray Witch cried.

When the witch and her minions had been vanished the three of them looked up in surprise. Diane grabbed the scroll and was surprised to see words now etched into the scroll. You have ended the rule of the Gray Witch. Earth will be protected by any other forms of evil by your power: Friendship. Spread this power to others. You have done your mission. Well done, Fairy Community.

"It worked!" they all exclaimed in unison.

"You did it! You are the destined ones." Carol and Dean shouted. Diane smiled and hugged them both back. "No, you're both wrong, we all are the destined ones." she exclaimed.

Epilogue

Years passed and the three friends still remember their adventure together. Dean, Carol, and Diane still have a strong bond that will last forever. As for the witch, she was banished to another realm where she was locked up for eternity to keep humankind safe. I will go back to when Diane sees her mother again.

"Mum?" Diane called. Her mother was crouched behind a potted plant and looked frightened. "What happened here while I was gone?"

Diane asked politely. "There was a terrible storm and two creatures were locking people up!" her mother exclaimed. Diane led her mother into the house where they shared their intake of the storm. Until a loud knock from outside caused them to be afraid. "W-who is it?" Diane uttered.

When no answer came in return she peeked open the door and peered out. "Darling!" her father, Maximus cried in joy. "Dad!" Diane exclaimed. The three of them settled by the fireplace and talked all evening long.

ROBERT REILEY
BIOGRAPHY

Robert Reiley was born in Virginia and currently lives in Charlotte, North Carolina. He attends Hawk Ridge Elementary and will be going into the fourth grade this fall. Robert lives with his parents, brother and dog. Robert Reiley has written Hershey and Mister: Food Alive and The Story of Bree Ann. He hopes to be a basketball player as an adult.

HERSHEY AND MISTER: FOOD ALIVE

By Robbie Reiley

I dedicate my story to Mrs. Miller's class.

Chapter 1

On a hot, hot summer day, my robot dog Mustache Man and I were practicing football outside and he threw the ball right smack dab in the middle of the pillow I wear taped to my head.

"Ow! That really hurt!" I said.

"Sorry about that. I didn't mean to hit you," he apologized. "Hey, are you as hungry as I am? It's after two o'clock. Let's go eat!"

So, my dog and I went inside my house. "Hmmm, what we can eat?" I wondered aloud. I reached in the frig for a lemon, since they go great with anything. Weird thing, though! I went to sit down at the table, picked up the lemon, and just as I was going to put it in my mouth, it started to shake! Then it grew arms

and legs and a face!

"Don't eat me!" The lemon was shouting at me!

I let out a scream that could be heard down the block.

"AHHHHHHH!" I took a deep breath and screamed

some more. "AHHHHHHHHH!" Even as I screamed, the

lemon just stared at me. Then, before you could say

strunkadoodle, the lemon vanished."

That was so weird," I said to Mustache Man. "I wonder

how that even happened?"

Mustache Man stood with his metal jaw open. "Did you

just see what happened? Mom's gonna kill us!!"

"It didn't even leave a mess to clean up," I pointed out.

"Don't be a worry wart."

When it was time for dinner, I grabbed a taco. Guess

what? The same thing

happened with the taco as happened with the lemon. It

came to life! But this time, I managed to grab it and ask it

some questions.

"How are you coming to life?" I demanded.

I saw the taco's mouth open wide then close—open then

close—until it finally tried to say something.

Unfortunately, I couldn't understand it. Was it speaking

another language or something?

Chapter 2

The next morning I refused to eat breakfast. I was afraid!

I also didn't play cards with Mustache Man as usual or

even get out of bed. I couldn't stop thinking about my

terrifying experience the day before. Mustache Man and I

stayed put.

When Mom called us for breakfast, we didn't even bother going downstairs.

" Hershey! What are you guys doing up there?" she called to me a second time.

My robot friend answered her. "I'll fix Hershey some breakfast in a few minutes."

He was always a quick thinker. He knew Mom would be off to work soon and neither of us would have to go down the stairs at all.

"Okay," she answered. "Just don't forget to eat!" When Mom had gone, I got ready for the day. I didn't have to change since I wear the same clothes every day, but I did add a couple of layers of glasses for the best possible eyesight and I pulled on extra socks since having warm feet makes me feel less nervous.

Soon it was time for lunch. Still I refused to go downstairs. Instead Mustache Man and I thought and thought. We needed clues that would help us figure out what was making the food come alive. We searched and searched and searched until we found it—the most evil thing in the world! Inside an upstairs closet we found a giant hot dog!

"It was you, wasn't it?" I accused the oversized lunch.

"Actually, Rotten Robby did it!" the hot dog confessed.

" Who is Rotten Robby?" asked Mustache Man.

" Me!" said the hot dog. Then it began to cry. "I was jealous of your robot dog and wanted to scare him away!"

Well, that just made me mad, so I decided Rotten Robby had to go. So you know what I did? I ATE him! I was so hungry from not eating that I grabbed everything I could find in the refrigerator. That's when I realized that all the food had returned to normal again! That made me so happy that it gave me an idea. In the fall, Mustache Man and I set up an awesome hot dog stand for those who are hungry.

A boy and his dog can do anything!

OLIVIA PACINI
BIOGRAPHY

Olivia Pacini is 9 years old and is in 4th grade. She is from Cleveland, Ohio but currently lives in Charlotte, North Carolina with her parents, her younger sister, Stella and her younger brother, Jackson.

Olivia wants to be an author when she grows up. In her free time she likes to play with her siblings and friends, and loves to write stories, draw and dance.

ALICE HOLMES AND THE UNSOLVED CASE

By Olivia Pacini

Prologue: 4 Hours Before

A shape moved toward the girl in the bed. The girl's eyes
fluttered. The shape stopped moving. When it was sure
that the girl was fully asleep, it moved beside the bed.
Then it pulled out something. It glittered in the
moonlight. Then the girl's eyes opened wide this

time, and she screamed. Everything went black. The
shape disappeared.

Chapter #1

"Mother, what's wrong?" asked Alice.

Alice is a twelve-year old girl who really wants to solve
mysteries, though she's not really good at it. She has

brown hair and freckles and the curiosity that ran through her family. Her mother is Enola Holmes and her uncle is Sherlock Holmes.

"Honey, something happened last night. I just heard the news," Alice's mother said as she rushed out the door.

Alice ran after her. Her bare feet hit the cobblestone street so hard that Alice's feet got cuts and bruises. She could faintly smell the normal London scent: fresh peanuts, fruit and smoke. Alice stared at the house, her heart beating wildly.

"Alice, be careful and don't touch ANYTHING," Alice's mother hissed.

They walked into the house. The floor was velvet and the walls golden. It had a grand staircase with hardwood. That was something that the Holmes Family didn't have, despite all the money Alice's uncle made. Alice recognized her friend, Emily Watson's house right away.

Are Emily and her sister okay? What could be wrong? Why would we be here for a mystery?

"Mother, why are we here?" Alice asked, suspiciously.

"You'll see," Alice's mother said carefully, as if she wasn't sure whether to tell Alice or not, "We have to go upstairs," she continued.

They walked up the stairs.

"Ah, Detective Holmes. So glad you're here," exclaimed a man. He had brown eyes, bushy eyebrows, a gray mustache, and gray hair.

"Honey, say hello to Mr. Watson," Alice's mother said, sadly.

Mr. Watson was wiping his eyes.

"You can go investigate her room," he sobbed.

Alice and her mother walked into the girl's room. Inside the room was a mess. The bedcovers were all messed up, and there was something red on the sheets. Then on the other side of the room was a box filled with fingerprint powder and a brush and something that looked like a stick with inches on it for measuring footprints.

Something must have happened to Anne! Oh no! What happened?

" Um, Mr. Watson, where is Anne's body?" Alice's mother asked.

"What?" Alice asked in shock.

"Oh, another detective took her for further investigation," he responded.

"Alice, you need to go home with your uncle," her mother said, firmly.

"Mother, I'm 12! I can help you solve mysteries!"

"Alice," her mother said in an angry tone.

When Alice walked home, she saw a dark shape descending down a dark alley.

Chapter #2

The boy pulled off his mask. Then his gloves. He noticed something in one of the gloves. A hole. The boy growled with anger, fear and shame. He was going to be caught. He went outside of the secret room in the alley, ready for revenge.

Chapter #3

Alice moved toward the alley, unaware of the boy watching her. Doyle Moriarty, the boy, moved closer to Alice. His beady eyes following her every move. Alice looked around. She suddenly felt eyes watching her. She felt as if his eyes were blazing right through her.

Doyle was watching Alice so he could try to track her family down. Then she saw Doyle. She remembered her uncle saying: 'Stay away from Doyle. He's vicious. Stay away.' Alice knew who Doyle was. She turned and ran.

Chapter #4

Doyle, frustrated, walked back into his "hideout". He was really mad. His father was going to be even angrier. He had let her escape. James Moriarty wasn't a big fan of his son failing or making mistakes. James wanted Sherlock Holmes GONE.

"Father, I'm sorry. I let the girl get away. I made a mistake. Just PLEASE father. Let me try again."

A man stepped out of the shadows. He had grey hair and a mustache. James Moriarty.

Chapter #5

Alice tossed and turned all night. She had weird dreams of Doyle Moriarty. He was repeatedly screaming, "You need to be gone." Then Alice knew. Her mother and uncle needed help. They needed her. They still hadn't gotten any clues on the case. Alice stuck on her robe and boots, then hurried across the street to the house where the girl was murdered. She went to the back of the house and pushed open the secret door in the wall that was covered with ivy. She remembered when she and Emily had played and they discovered the door. Coincidentally, it led to Emily's sister's room. She climbed up the ladder that led to the room. She pushed open the secret trapdoor. Then she noticed a tuft of wool inside of the hinge of the trapdoor. She took out her powder and brush and dusted for fingerprints. Then she saw a fingerprint. Doyle Moriarty's fingerprint to be exact. Then a hand covered Alice's mouth and pulled her off the ladder and carried her into darkness. Now nobody would know who

the murderer was. Nobody.

ABBEY SOUROV
BIOGRAPHY

Abbey Sourov is a fourth grader who lives in Seattle, WA with her family. She enjoys reading, writing and swimming. When she grows up she would like to be an author or an actress.

<u>HEROES</u>

By Abbey Sourov

Dedicated to the best teacher ever, Mrs. Mansfield, who

helped me improve my writing.

The riverbank. That's where I saw it. The thing that

changed my life forever. That slip of paper. I just had

to pick it up and read it. How was I supposed to know it

would unleash an evil sorceress?

I had no idea I'd end up in a cage with my friend Amelia,

but we'll get to that later. My name is Jason by the way.

Now, I'll tell you how I met Amelia, and how my life

took a very wrong turn. Be prepared, you might want to

run off screaming I'm crazy.

I was walking home from school with my buddy, Eric.

"I'm gonna take the shortcut through the

riverbank. See you later?" I said to Eric.

Eric shrugged. "Sure. See you later Jason." He waved and headed in the other direction.

I was halfway across the riverbank when I saw a flicker of light near my foot. It was a piece of paper. I unfolded it and read, *"Rise Meshani."* The wind howled but nothing else happened.

"What the heck does that mean?" I muttered as I stuffed it in my pocket. When I got home, I saw a girl waiting on the porch. She had black curly hair and dark skin. And she wore a tank top over jeans. Her arms were crossed, and she was glaring right at me. Before I could say anything she said rudely, "What did you do?"

(Okay, if some weird stranger asks you something, you probably shouldn't reply, but I wasn't thinking.)

"Uh, what?" I asked.

"Ugh! Did you read anything, like, out of the ordinary?" she groaned. She looked me in the eyes. Hers were bright green. She read my expression. "Oh no," she mumbled. Then she backed away from me.

"Who are you and what did I do?" I yelled.

"I'm Amelia," she snapped. "And you just unleashed an evil sorceress."

"How is that possible?" I whispered.

"It just is. She`s the mother of all monsters, and she`s trying to take over the universe."

I didn't say anything. Finally I could speak again. "What can we do?" I asked.

"I'll show you." And Amelia headed toward a couple of boulders. She literally walked through them. No, seriously. She just walked into the rocks. And I followed her.

"Whoa." It was amazing. The walls of the cave were filled with gleaming jewels and stones.

"Come on." Amelia led me through the cave until we were in a dark room with a round circle of metal on the floor.

"What`s that?" I asked.

"It`s a portal. It will take us to the sorceress, Meshani," she answered.

"Um, do we want that?"

"Yes," she said like it was obvious. "If we know where she is, we can stop her."

"So, we just jump in?" I asked. Amelia shrugged. I jumped and she followed.

It felt like diving into a pool... without the water. But it only lasted for a second. Then I was in a dark cavern, with Amelia beside me. Then a whispering voice echoed around the cavern.

"I am Meshani. And I'm so happy you could join us." Then the cave brightened and a woman wearing an evil grin surrounded by monsters appeared. This is the point where I and Amelia are trapped in a cage.

"What do we do?" Amelia whispered.

"I don't know. You're the one who knows about this sorceress!" I whispered back.

"Oh. I-I don't have a plan," Amelia said.

I looked around. "Actually I do have one idea," I told Amelia. I whispered the plan.

"Hey!" Amelia yelled at the monster that was guarding us. The monster growled at her. Then Amelia started shouting about how bad his breath is, and while the monster's attention was on Amelia, I found a rock and started sawing at the cage. After I made a space big enough for a person, I crept out. The monster turned, but before he could yell, I threw the rock at him and knocked him unconscious.

"Your plan actually worked," Amelia said.

I grinned. "Yeah, Now what?"

"We need to give Meshani a talking to," Amelia snarled.

We turned a corner and Amelia peeked around.

"Anyone there?" I asked.

"Shhh!" she hissed. I peeked around the corner. In the middle of the room was Meshani surrounded by thousands of monsters. We tiptoed into the room.

"Wait!" Amelia whispered. "Look!" I looked down. On the floor was a gold medal.

"What`s that?" I asked.

"A magical medal. We need to get this around her neck." Amelia pointed at Meshani.

"How?" Amelia whispered a crazy plan to me. "I hope this works," I muttered.

As we had hoped, Meshani noticed us. Her red eyes narrowed as she screamed, "There! Get them!" She charged, followed by the monsters. But at that second, Amelia handed me the medal and jumped out of the way.

I jumped, just as Meshani was about to grab me and then slipped the magical medal across her neck.

Meshani just had time to yell, "No! I was so close!" before disappearing in black smoke. And with her, so did the monsters.

Amelia and I just stood there in silence until I whispered, "We did it." Then I shouted, "We did it!" We hugged and cheered. When we stopped I said, "Amelia, how do we get back home?" She thought for a minute. Her eyes scanned the room. She stared at a clump of boulders. She touched the boulders and walked through it and once again, I followed her.

Once we walked to my house, we stopped in the yard. Amelia turned to me and said, "Well, bye."

I grinned. "Yeah, nice fighting monsters with you."

She smiled. "Yeah." She hugged me.

The next day I saw somebody standing outside.

"Amelia?" I asked.

"Of course."

"Why are you here? Do we have some monsters to fight?"

She grinned, "Uh huh."

I smiled. "Let's do this." And we ran off laughing, planning our next adventure.

ELLE OCHENAS

BIOGRAPHY

Elle is a seventh grade student in North Carolina. In addition to writing she enjoys drawing, Minecraft and watching all Aphmau videos. Her favorite meal is steak with chimichurri.

The Fallen Are Rising

By Elle Ochenas

I open my eyes. Dirt and stone. Yes! My hibernation must be over! I can finally rejoin the human world! *Man, a couple thousand years of hibernation can really stiffen up the joints!*

"Sheni! Sheni, wake up! Our banishment is over! Wake up Gecko!" Sheni is my dragon companion, she's always so serious! She hates being called 'Gecko' too, so she should be-

"Don't *ever* call me Gecko!" She screeches, leaping up and biting my ears.

"Come on," I say, "Let's go see if humans have figured out how to keep animals from going extinct yet!" I push my way out from under the mountain. Just as I poke my head out, a metal monster rushes by on a path of darkness! I quickly duck back underground, looking at Sheni, her yellow scales glowing slightly in the darkness.

"What was that thing?" I ask her, scared.

"I don't know any better than you" She obviously doesn't know the danger we could be in! I peek out again, and thankfully the monster is gone. I call a falcon down to help us. As he lands, I ask him,

"What was that monster?"

"What monster?" Falcon replies.

"The great metal one on the path of darkness, of course!" I exclaim.

"Wow, the gods really are getting dumber." He mutters. "That was a *car* and the 'path of darkness' is a *road*." He explains exasperatedly.

"I'm not dumb, I've just been hibernating for two millennia!" I reply indignantly. I am the Earth God. How dare he speak to me that way?

"W-wait... You're not... the Earth god that... that the Gods banished long ago... are you?" Falcon stammers. "I thought that was just a myth!"

"Of course I am! Couldn't you tell by my aura?" I ask, confused.

"You're bad news! See you never!" He yells, already in the air.

"Sheni, what was that about?" I turn to her.

"Well, you did try to imprison the Sky God for turning penguins' arms to wings. They look better with wings anyways!"

"Well, that makes sense. You're right." I say. "Time to find civilization! But first... embrace your inner gecko! The humans can't know you're a dragon."

"Grrrr... Fine" Sheni growls, hiding her wings. She climbs onto my shoulder, and we start walking.

*   *   *

"Sheni, look at the buildings!" I gasp, "They're like *mountains*! I can barely see the top!"

"Yes, very big. Now get me food, I haven't eaten in two thousand years and three days." Sheni hisses at me, scowling. *Come to think of it, I'm a bit peckish too,* I think.

"Squish's Hot Dogs, heaven in your mouth. Come and get it." A man says flatly nearby. The first things I notice about him are his clothes. They are like a colorful toga, split in two! How odd. I look down at my pale brown toga, and decide to change it into something similar to his.

I snap my fingers, and I'm wearing a light green top toga and a dull blue bottom toga. They feel so strange! *Humans have changed so much!* I start to walk into 'Squish's Hot Dogs', but the man stops me.

"Sorry dude, no pets." He tells me, not seeming to have noticed my sudden change of clothes.

"What do you mean, pet?" I reply, a bit confused.

"The gecko." Sheni digs her claws into my shoulder. "Ditch it and you can go in." He says, exasperated. I pat my small companion in an attempt to calm her down. I turn away from the building, when an amazing smell hits me. I follow it behind the building, and see a green box. It must be meant for me!

"Sheni, look! An entire box of food!" I pick up a piece of strange meat and eat some.

"Is it good? Can I eat now?" Sheni asks impatiently.

"Yes, this is amazing!" I say in wonder, giving her a bite. Her eyes light up, and she dives into the box. A few minutes after I finish my meat, Sheni resurfaces with a large black bag full of pieces of meat.

"Look at this!" She exclaims, nudging the bag. "It's completely full!" She smiles. As I dig in, I hear a woman exclaim. I look up and see her speaking into a tiny box.

"Yes, thief behind Squish's Hot Dogs on North Main Street!" She howls. *Thief? I'm no thief!*

"Ma'am, I'm no thief-" I begin to say.

"Stay where you are! I have pepper spray!" She says, looking terrified. *What's pepper spray?* I wonder. I hear birds screaming, louder and louder, and suddenly, two 'cars' trap me! A man hops out of one and says,

"Hands up thief! Return what you've stolen from this woman!" He orders, pointing a small contraption at me.

"What? No human can command the God of-" I hiss, but he cuts me off.

"I said hands up! I am armed!" He says, angry. I grudgingly put my hands up, playing along. "Get in the car, you have the right to remain silent," He tells me. Sheni climbs onto my shoulder, eyes wide.

"You can't make me go in the monster!" I yell, growing a vine up the side of a building.

"We've got a crazy one." The man says into a tiny box.

The vine finishes growing, and I begin to climb it as quickly as possible. I reach the top and the vine wilts, falling to the ground.

"That was too close!" Sheni yells at me, upset. "Now the 'Charlotte Police' are after us!"

"How do you know those were 'Charlotte Police'?" I ask.

"It said so on the cars!" She replies. "Maybe that means this place is called Charlotte, too?" She wonders.

"Maybe." I reply.

*   *   *

A couple of days ago we fled Charlotte, and now we've reached the Town of Mooresville. It's so small compared to Charlotte! The buildings are like mansions though! We've found an abandoned house so stay in. It's quite cozy, actually!

"I'm hungry!" Sheni nags. I pull two pieces of meat from a pocket in my bottom toga.

"When did you…" Sheni asks.

"I grabbed them when you weren't looking." I reply simply. I hand her her pice of meat, and she eats it quickly. I finish mine a few minutes later.

We talk for a little while, but sleep takes over and we aren't able to stay awake for long. We will need our rest for the long days ahead in this new world.

ANN MARGARET SPROUL
BIOGRAPHY

Ann Margaret Sproul, age 10, is a fifth grade student at New Hope Elementary School in Gastonia, NC. Ann Margaret is a Christian intrigued by other cultures. She is currently working on a novel, The Kingdom of Twelve. Ann Margaret's favorite pastimes include art, creative writing, reading, skiing and playing with her friends. Ann Margaret lives with her parents and brother in Cramerton, NC.

HUNTERS OF ARTEMIS

By Ann Margaret Sproul

Rachel, daughter of Athena, was born on Mt. Olympus in front of all the gods. Hestia and Artemis helped her mother through labor. Rachel was conceited and spoiled, but she was fun to be around. Zeus let her ride Pegasus and, by the time she was five, Rachel knew she wanted to be a Hunter of Artemis.

The Hunters of Artemis were a group of Olympus-worthy girls who hunted monsters. At age eleven, she approached Artemis. They went back and forth, but Artemis won. Rachel ran to Apollo, crying.

"What is wrong, dear child?" Apollo asked.

"Artemis won't let me join the Hunt," Rachel sobbed.

"Go to Delphi," commanded Apollo, fading into the sun.

Rachel went to the Oracle. He commanded her to slay monsters to prove herself worthy. She asked Zeus if it was alright. "Don't let things get too out of hand or you'll be back to Olympus before you can say 'Chimera slayer.'"

Rachel put on armor and strapped a knife to her belt, along with some rope. She slung her bow and arrow on her shoulder and put two spears on her back. As she was leaving, she decided to put some Ambrosia on her belt.

The first monster she met was a sea monster. She cursed Poseidon for not watching his turf and drove her spear into his throat. It didn't make a dent in his strong scales, though, and he swallowed her.

When she woke up, she drank some Ambrosia. She decided she would rot inside of the monster's throat when he swallowed the grossest thing she had ever seen. Rachel thought it was a deformed octopus. It had twelve long tentacles, a squishy body and a white tail and uneven holes for ears. That is when she decided that she couldn't stay, so she took her spear and charged out.

The next time she encountered monsters, she was smarter. She encountered a band of monsters this time: one long scaly python, five giants (each twelve feet tall) and twelve hellhounds.

Rachel climbed a tree and whistled for Pegasus. From there, she shot at the Python, which, unfortunately, only angered it. Rachel knew a knot she could use, like a lasso, that would allow her to tighten the rope and strangle the Python.

She went down and started the knot. The giants were closing in on her. Her fingers were flashing. "Up, Pegasus," she commanded.

Pegasus shot up in the air. Rachel could feel the strain in the rope. "Higher!" Rachel's hands burned, but she held on. Rachel could see the snake disintegrating.

"Come on, come on." She could hardly stand the burning. The rope went slack. The python was dead. "Pegasus, we did it. Let's go lower so we can shoot the other monsters."

That part was easy. She shot each giant and the hellhounds with a flaming arrow. Then, she and Pegasus flew to Olympus.

Rachel wasn't greeted with the normal faces of the smiling guards. She was greeted with putrid breath, pig-like snouts and claws. Rachel wouldn't have any of that. She killed them each with her knife. She marched up to the throne room. All the gods were tied up. She untied them all, making a point to untie Artemis last. Artemis growled in reaction.

"Watch it, girlie. I didn't have to save your life," Rachel warned.

"You will do as we command," Zeus ordered.

"Well, it's your life at stake, not mine," Rachel responded sassily.

"Actually, child…" began Athena, "We cannot die. But, if you were in a situation where we could not help you, you would die."

"Shut up," Rachel mumbled. Athena glared at her and Rachel felt electric shock run through her body.

"Such disrespect will not be tolerated," Zeus ordered.

"May I join the hunt now?", Rachel asked Artemis, who told her no, which caused Rachel to sulk more.

Rachel killed all the monsters in Olympus that day, but the next day, they returned. She discovered the gods were hiding under a volcano.

"Why did they come back to life?" Rachel questioned.

Apollo shrugged and responded, "Ask Hades."

"Absolutely not," Zeus responded.

"But Zeus, you can't hide under this volcano forever," said Rachel realistically.

"I will send one of my priests, the great grandson of Hercules," said Zeus. When Rachel suggested he would be too weak, Zeus insisted. The priest was killed because Charon wouldn't let him pass.

Rachel asked again, "Now can I go?" Zeus scowled in response, but Hera stepped in, placing a hand on Zeus' shoulder, "Perhaps we should let the girl go. Every hero needs a chance to prove themselves."

With that, Rachel was sent to the underworld. Zeus accompanied her to the gate and ordered Charon to allow her to enter.

Rachel immediately approached Hades. "Monsters are escaping Tataurus. Why are you permitting this?"

Hades responded slyly, "I bargained with them.

You see, if I let them escape, they agreed to take over Olympus for me. Unfortunately, I can't allow you to snitch to Zeus, can I? I don't think Persephone would like that. You see, Demeter and I are good friends."

"Well, she doesn't have to now, does she?" Rachel starts to yell, but Hades points to her and she goes quiet. "Would you like something to eat? Perhaps a pomegranate?" Rachel shakes her head vigorously, but Hades points to her and she stops – a pomegranate in hand. She puts it to her mouth and starts chewing. "Good girl. Do you like it? It's a product of the underworld." Hades closes his eyes. Rachel marches up to him and spits it in his face, "Sorry, but I hated it."

Rachel angrily returns to the volcano. "Hades released them," she growled. "What happened?" Zeus asked. She explains what happened. Demeter asks, "Did he try to get you to eat something." Rachel nods, "but I spit it in his face. C'mon, we have to go." "No, Demeter will go to the underworld. The rest of you will go fight the remaining monsters. You have angered Hades. Stay here," orders Zeus.

"But Zeus, I want to fight! Let me help save Olympus!," Rachel exclaimed.

"You already have," responded Zeus, coldly. A flash of light and the Olympians were gone. Gone, taking with them Rachel's dream.

She looked around to see where she was. The cells of her prison, where she would stay out of the way. Rachel curled into a ball and cried herself to sleep.

When Rachel woke, a dim lantern lit the room. "You can come out now." Rachel looked up and saw Hestia. "You know, you did Olympus a big favor," Hestia comforted Rachel. Hestia was good at comforting but Rachel's heart was broken.

"I wanted to fight. I'm twelve. You should have let me fight." Rachel's voice echoed off the stone walls.

"You would have died," said Hestia, gently.

They continued in silence.

Athena and Artemis met her at the steps of

Olympus. "Rachel, my beautiful daughter," Athena

cooed, stroking Rachel's cheek.

"Yes, one definitely worthy of my hunt," Artemis

smiled.

"I can join?" asked Rachel, perking up.

"Of course you may. You have proven yourself

worthy," responded Artemis.

Made in the USA
Lexington, KY
24 September 2017